For Pì

Tundra Books, an imprint of Penguin Random House Canada Young Readers,
a division of Penguin Random House of Canada Limited

Library and Archives Canada Cataloguing in Publication

Title: The boy and the mountain / Mario Bellini ; Marianna Coppo, illustrator.
Names: Bellini, Mario, 1983- author. | Coppo, Marianna, illustrator.
Identifiers: Canadiana (print) 20210109092 | Canadiana (ebook) 20210109106
ISBN 9780735270251 (hardcover) | ISBN 9780735270268 (EPUB)
Subjects: LCGFT: Picture books.
Classification: LCC PZ7.1.B45 Bo 2022 | DDC j823/.92—dc23

Published simultaneously in the United States of America by Tundra Books of
Northern New York, an imprint of Penguin Random House Canada Young Readers,
a division of Penguin Random House of Canada Limited

Library of Congress Control Number: 2020952414

Edited by Peter Phillips
Acquired by Tara Walker
Translated by Debbie Bibo
Designed by John Martz
The artwork in this book was rendered in gouache and finished digitally.
The text was set in TT Norms.

Printed in China

www.penguinrandomhouse.ca

1 2 3 4 5   26 25 24 23 22

tundra

Penguin
Random House
TUNDRA BOOKS

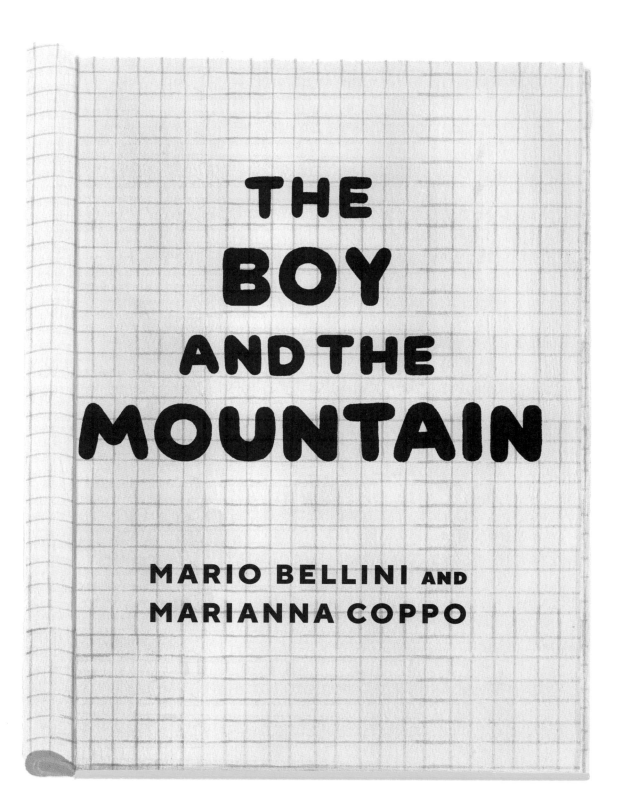

THE
BOY
AND THE
MOUNTAIN

MARIO BELLINI AND
MARIANNA COPPO

tundra

There once was a boy who always looked at a mountain.

He would say good morning
to the mountain when he woke up

and say good night to it before he went to bed.

One day, the boy decided to draw the mountain.

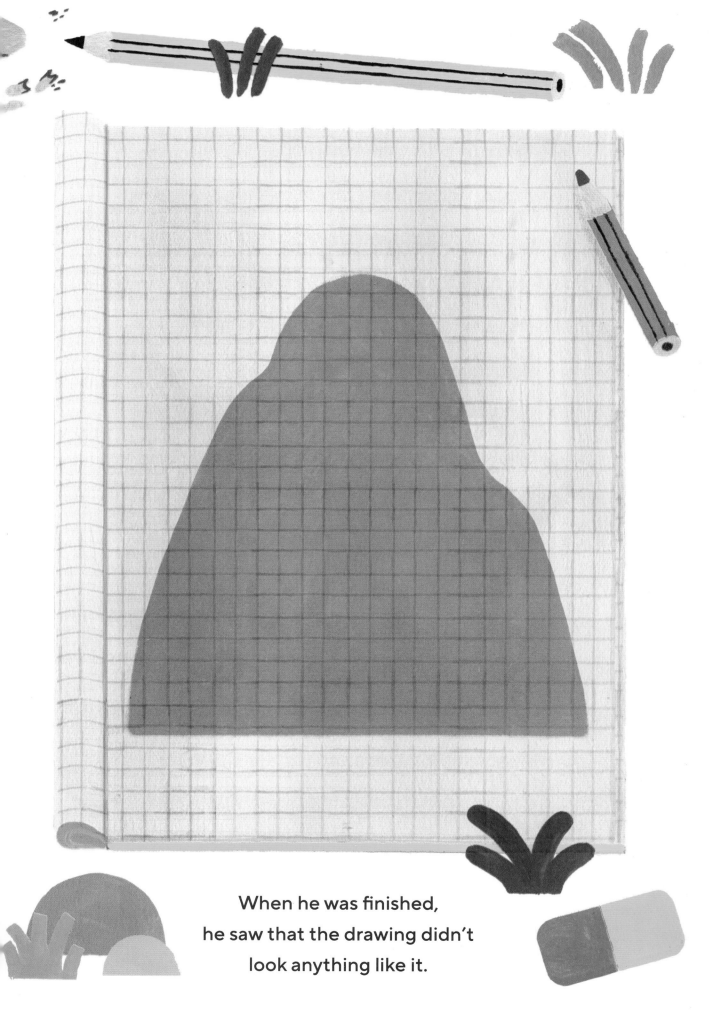

When he was finished,
he saw that the drawing didn't
look anything like it.

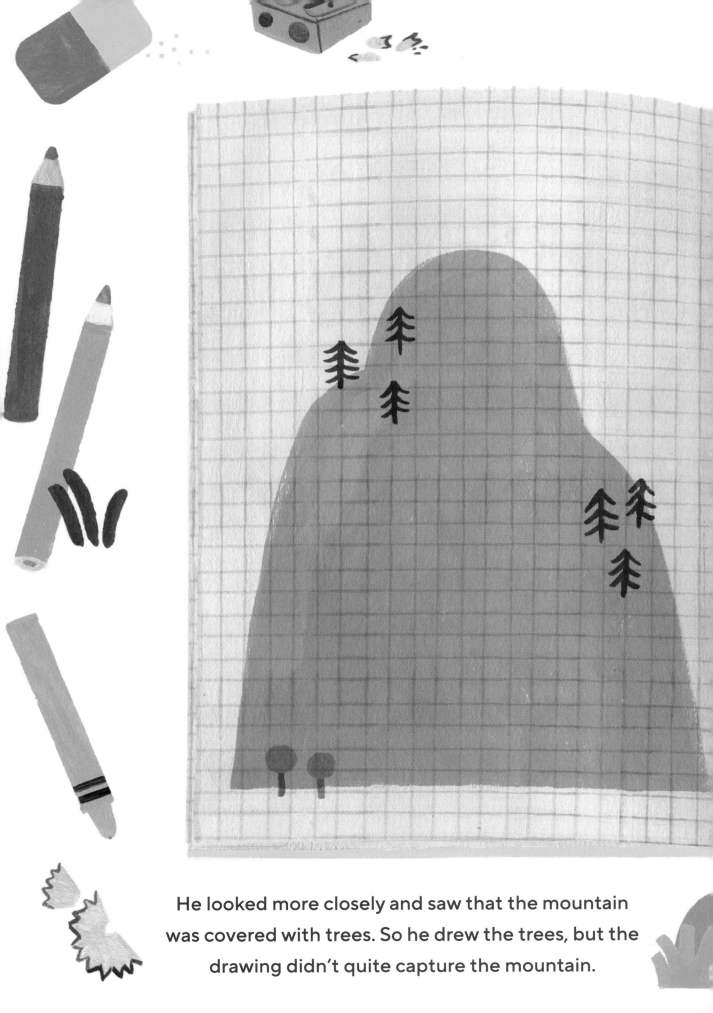

He looked more closely and saw that the mountain was covered with trees. So he drew the trees, but the drawing didn't quite capture the mountain.

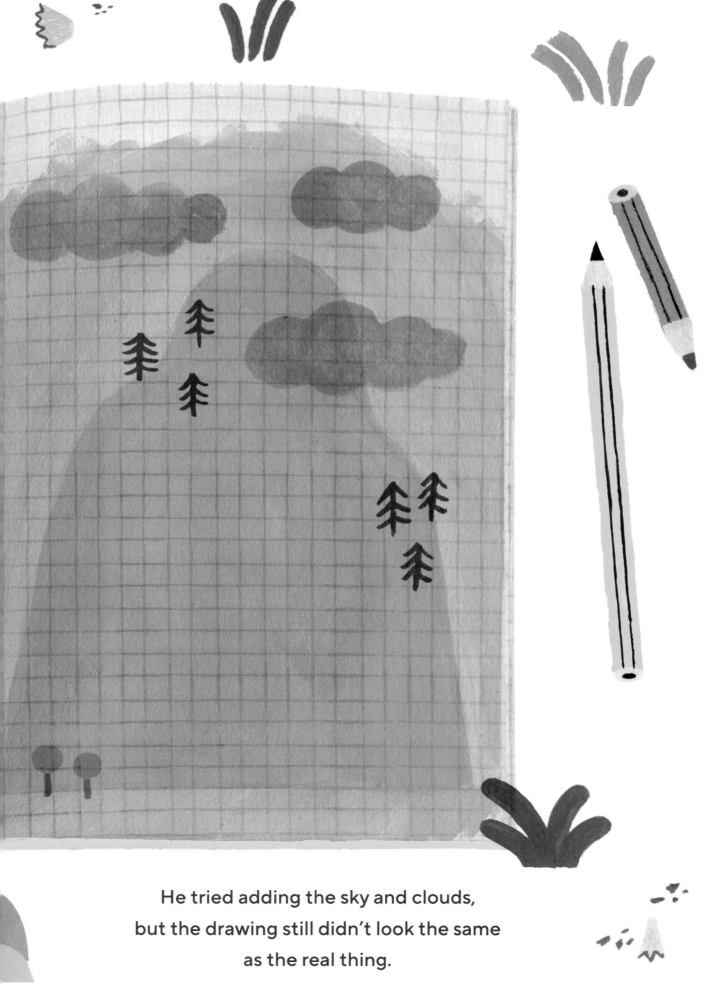

He tried adding the sky and clouds,
but the drawing still didn't look the same
as the real thing.

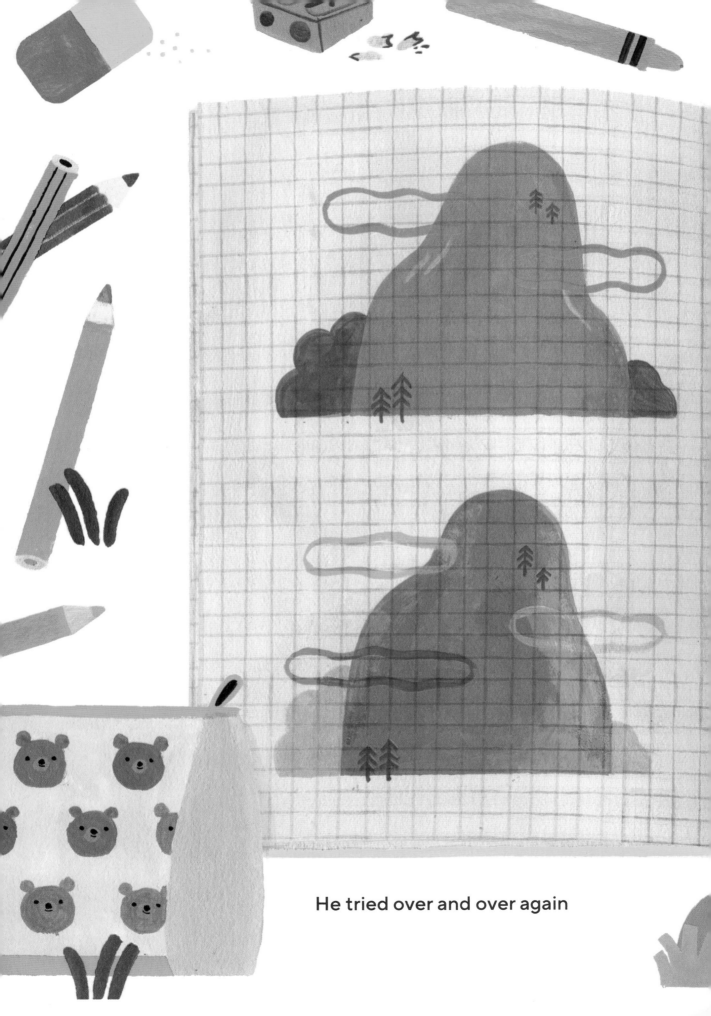

He tried over and over again

but was never happy with what he had drawn.

So the boy decided to
take an even closer look.

On the way up to the mountain,
he saw a goat and drew it.

The goat liked the drawing a lot.

Then the boy spotted some birds.

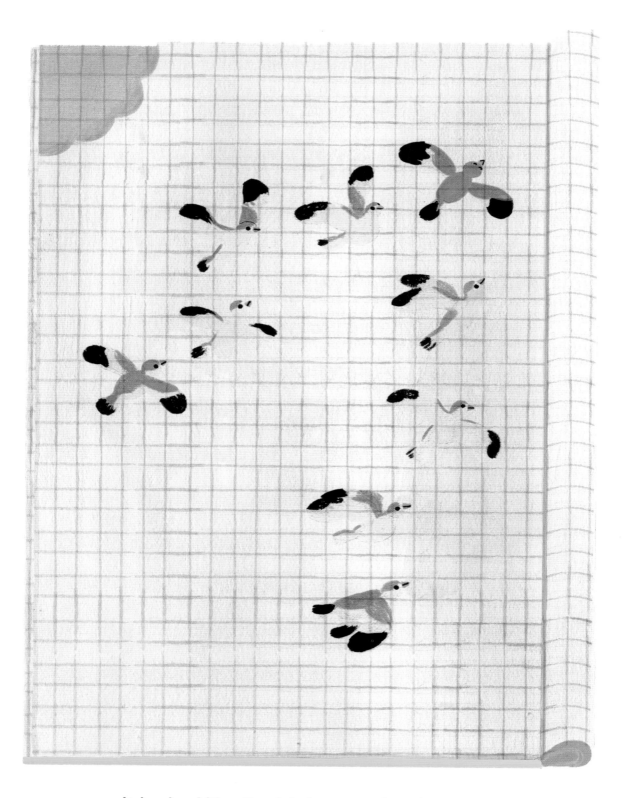

It looked like the birds were drawing, too.

He reached a stream
and drew it,

but the drawing didn't turn out very well.

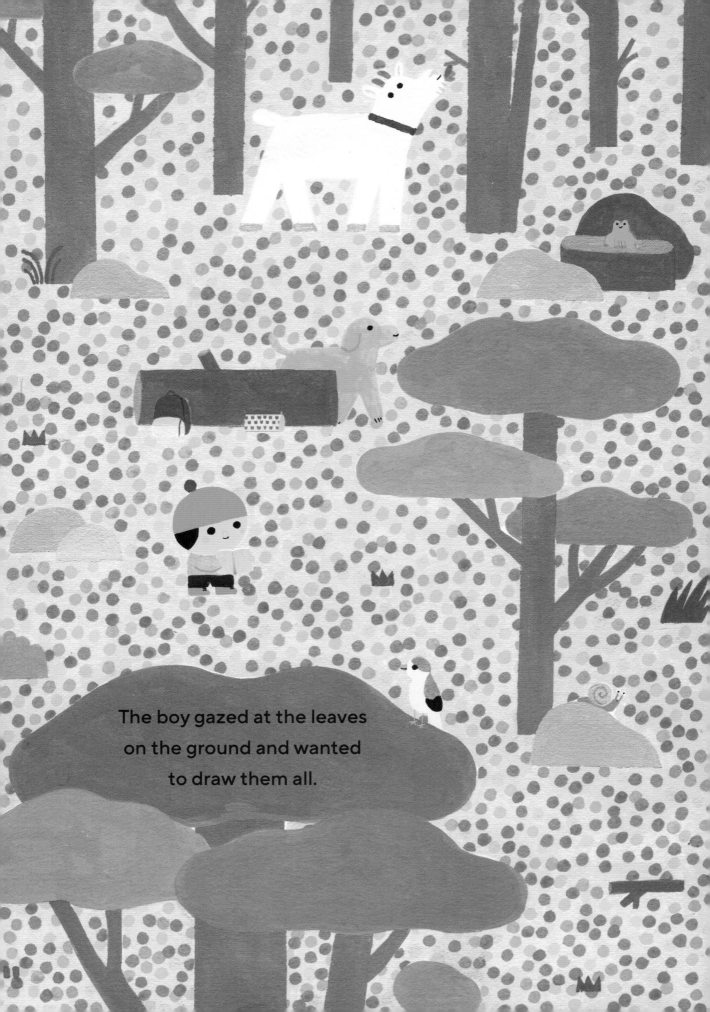

The boy gazed at the leaves
on the ground and wanted
to draw them all.

He realized that even though the leaves were small,
there wasn't enough room for all of them.

Suddenly,
the mountain disappeared.

It was only hiding.

The boy climbed some more

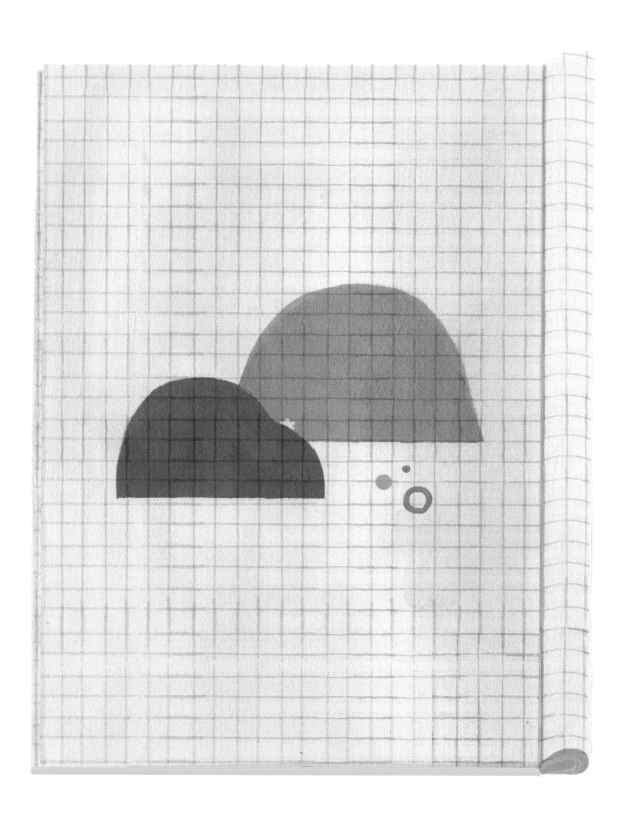

and saw that there wasn't much left to draw.

Until he looked more closely.

Without even noticing,
he had reached the peak.

The boy sat to take in the view
and look at all the drawings he had made.

He thought there was still something missing.

"Ohhh . . . hello!"
said the boy.

Time flew by that afternoon.

"See you soon!" said the boy.

That night, before he said good night to the mountain,
the boy drew it once more.

And, this time,
he was completely
satisfied.